# Ivan and the Silver Seeds

# Ivan and the Silver Seeds

ISBN 978-0-578-87505-7

# Ivan and the Silver Seeds

Ivy Lin
Walter Sattazahn Jr.

Papa Owl smiles as he holds something shiny.

"10 silver seeds for each of you this summer!"

"Hooooooohooooo!!!!"
Ivan and his brother Ryan hoot with
excitement about the silver seeds.

Little Ivan dreams of
fiery comets and sparkling stars.

His big brother Ryan
dreams of a sugary world
made of chocolate cake
and sweet candy.

Maybe their dreams are waiting for them in town.

The brothers take
their silver seeds
to the local shops.

Ivan is surprised to find that he cannot buy a telescope.

Manny the shop owner looks at his 10 silver seeds and then points to the price tag.

"This telescope is 100 silver seeds!" he squawks.

"I don't have enough silver seeds,"
little Ivan cries. "What should I do?"

Papa Owl thinks for awhile as
he searches for ideas on his laptop...

Papa Owl's eyes grow big as he
remembers something.

"I have an idea!" he hoots.
"You can join the talent show
at the Aviary Fair!"

At the fair,
Ivan sees magicians, singers, and a bird in
green tights. He also sees pinwheels, balloons,
and colorful lights. The Aviary Talent Show is easy
to find, and he quickly signs up
with a performance in mind.

Greggy, the talent show host, waves at the crowd as he makes an announcement.

"Good evening, everyone!" he says with a honk.

"Tonight we have the greatest talent show in Aviary Town's history!"

Ivan waits for his turn
behind the big red curtain.

He feels a little nervous as he
listens to the loud squawking and
hooting of the crowd.

It is now
Ivan's turn!

His mind is focused as he paints his ideas
with glue onto a big black board.

The crowd is excited to see what will happen next!

They watch Ivan launch shiny, colorful glitter from his bucket onto the sticky glue painting!

The shiny, sparkling glitter reveals
Ivan's dream to the cheering crowd.

Ivan is happy to take part in a great
talent show and share his dream.

He has more experience and a prize
to help him get closer to his goal.

"I won 70 silver seeds at the talent show!"

The next day, Mama and Papa Owl give little Ivan an idea. He can plant gooseberry bushes!

The gooseberries can be used to make tasty pies, delicious muffins, and sweet jam to sell for more silver seeds.

A new adventure begins as Ivan plants 3 gooseberry bushes.

He waters the bushes to help them grow under the warm light of the sun.

Over time, the bushes grow bigger and bigger!

Now he can pick the juicy, red gooseberries!

Ivan is ready to make pies!

He rolls the dough flat
and cuts it into strips.

Then he carefully layers the strips
on top of the gooseberry filling.

Mama Owl helps by sharing
her pie recipe.

The gooseberry bake sale
is a success!

The local birds quickly spread the word about
Ivan's exciting new gooseberry bake sale.

"Mmmmm! That smells good!"
Ryan hoots.

Little Ivan is happy to
share a free sample with
his big brother.

Mama and Papa Owl are happy to see that little Ivan has finally earned enough silver seeds to buy a telescope.

"I would like to buy
a telescope please!"
hoots Ivan.

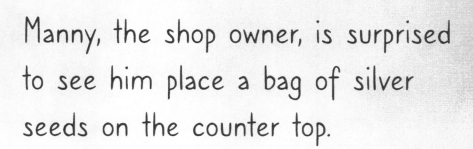

Manny, the shop owner, is surprised
to see him place a bag of silver
seeds on the counter top.

Ryan stares into the window
of the candy store as he eats
his last chocolate bar.

He wonders how he
will get more candy.

Ivan is filled with excitement as
he carries his first telescope in a big box.

Ryan follows behind as he pulls at some
pink bubblegum that is sticking to his feathers.

He starts to think that maybe he wants
something more than just candy.

Mama Owl helps Ivan assemble his telescope.

"There will be clear skies tonight!" she rejoices.
"Astronomers are saying that you can see a comet!"

Not far away, Papa Owl gives
Ryan some new ideas to leave his
bubble gum troubles behind.

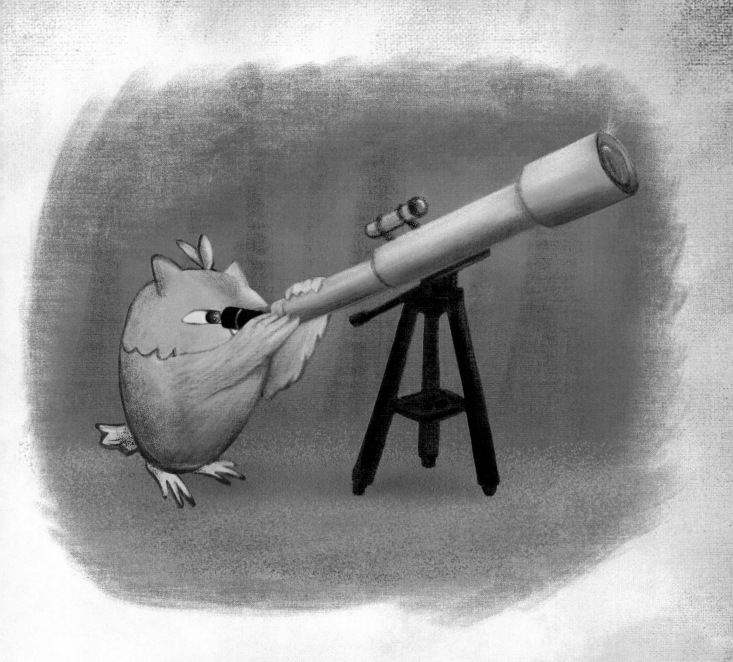

Ivan looks into the eyepiece and adjusts the telescope for a good view of the night sky.

Ivan can see the brilliant light of
a beautiful comet in the night sky.

Made in the USA
Middletown, DE
15 September 2021